THAT REMINDS ME

WITH

Derek Owusu is a writer, poet and podcaster from north London. He discovered his passion for literature at the age of twenty-three while studying exercise science at university. Unable to afford a change of degree, Derek began reading voraciously and sneaking into English Literature lectures at the University of Manchester. Derek edited and contributed to *Safe: On Black British Men Reclaiming Space*. *That Reminds Me*, his first solo work, won the Desmond Elliott Prize 2020.

Praise for *That Reminds Me*

'The book is a dreamy, impressionistic offering of reassembled fragments of memories emerging through the misty beauty of a deliciously individualistic poetic sensibility with flashes of Twi and UK London ebonics to further remind us of what has been missing from British poetry . . . I can't tell you how impressed I was and how much I enjoyed reading this stunning book.'
Bernardine Evaristo, author of *Girl, Woman, Other*

'*That Reminds Me* is a profoundly moving book about black bodies and identity, and about God, sex, family, art, love and madness. It is somehow both tender and unflinching, and the prose has both the lyricism of verse and the direct simplicity of overheard speech. Derek Owusu has made a vital contribution to the culture, and it should be widely read.'
Sarah Perry, author of *The Essex Serpent*

'This book is brave and moving . . . Owusu writes with an enlightening fluency.'
Observer, Poetry Book of the Month

THAT REMINDS ME

Derek Owusu

1 3 5 7 9 10 8 6 4 2

#Merky Books
20 Vauxhall Bridge Road
London SW1V 2SA

#Merky Books is part of the Penguin Random House group of companies
whose addresses can be found at global.penguinrandomhouse.com.

Penguin
Random House
UK

First published by #Merky Books in 2019
This paperback edition published by #Merky Books in 2020

www.penguin.co.uk

A CIP catalogue record for this book is available from the British Library.

ISBN 9781529118605

Typeset in 11.52/13.92 pt Minion Pro by Jouve (UK), Milton Keynes
Printed and bound in Great Britain by Clays Ltd, Elcograf S.p.A.

Penguin Random House is committed to a sustainable future for our business,
our readers and our planet. This book is made from Forest Stewardship
Council® certified paper.

For Berthy, whose friendship defies definition.
For Joel, for coming into my life
when I needed him most.
And Yomi, always for Yomi.

'To scathe walls of white and black,
it is the crime of the tainted man'
KALEKE KOLAWOLE

AUTHOR'S NOTE

This is the story of K. If you believe your life to be as fictitious as K's, if you find yourself within the pages of this book, then you are holding the pen and not me.

AWARENESS

Anansi, your four gifts raised to Nyame grant you no power over the stories I tell, stories that build like dew, alerting you but creating no music when they drop onto the drums of our sky. Take my 'gift', words bound in time, directly to him and tell me if his features betray recognition or sorrow.

He was the only one who didn't laugh. She stepped onto the escalator thinking it could sweep her away, swallow and shred her at the bottom. He would watch as she jumped off like a schoolgirl, brown skirt waving in his memory, and wait to see her smile rise like morning had begun, the shine of his morning cleaning. But her slow pace meant the last he saw of her was as she turned the corner of the underground and he was carried away by the indifference of the train. One evening he decided the strain of longing for love outweighed the strain of longing for home, so in the morning, after watching her nervous dance with the escalator, he stood in the middle of the train doors, arms wide holding them open, waiting for her. Turning the corner, she saw her Samson and ran towards him. It became their rite. Until train doors became bolted doors and Chubbs in the door of a flat. He loved her enough to turn off the lights before bed – though she could sleep with brightness, bills kept her awake. He took care of that too. She helped him become a man; let him use her calling card to speak to his mother while he pounded fufu, vigorous as he shook the stove. So maybe they kissed, maybe they laughed, maybe he did love my mum from the start.

My mum suffocated under the pool of light called an imperial sun, so my life begins with a nose broader than the wing on which I was weighed. But blessings are missed on the ward where wails are watered down by gasps of meconium. So to breathe (my mum thought) I needed to be streamlined. Without sense, my nose was pressured by two fingers to fit the box of Europe, the centre of my face growing close, comforting the holes in my appearance. Unknown abuse, I was being moulded for progress, a model given by God on which my mother could add the finishing touches – a joint project on which to project imbibed insecurities. So now I breathe British air with airs akin to royal heirs – my mum thought she was making a dark life fair.

Watch the little boy bobbing up and down on his father's lap, no one caring if he falls or where he'll land, and you'll think the boy has no chance, no way to change what's to become his life. His father wrote his destiny on the back of a betting slip, fixing it, and now he plays roulette with his boy watching the numbers, wondering what difference it makes where the ball settles. His father smacks his hand as he reaches for a button – he's not allowed to roll the dice or send the ball spinning, only an observer, black or red, eyes closed while he's winning.

London homes were closed to young, foreboding darkness, and so were the doors of a family letting go of the past. Once I'm in care, my mum occasionally picks me up but can't recall how I got there. There's six of us, three who soak their beds – me looking on thinking they're confused as to which way their tears should flow. And two who stand with me in the bathroom, water running but clothes still on, forced hands down my trousers. I learned to clip my nails daydreaming about my foster mother trimming hers, the cutting hurt, index and thumb pressed into my lobe when I misbehaved. Or there was a raised cane, a light cracking sound, no atmospheric stomach rumble as I think back, a white hand raised to strike black skin. How can the truth and my love not begin to lose synergy? So facile, it was all so easily flammable – the jet left, and my mum's hearty inhales, were enough to spark my curiosity, so I watched as my thumb gave rise to light, delivering the dissolving tissue to the plastic bin with our leftovers. There wasn't enough time for ashes to be born but I stepped back in awe of the flaming wings rising to the ceiling. The fire was out with air to spare – my foster mother's age containing a vitality that doused the flames, throwing a jug of water then taking me to the fridge. She held onto my arm while cutting a Scotch bonnet, then rubbed it into my face – to burn off that troublesome nose and the thick lips that talked back. I was in bed early and as I tried to sleep, the dripping tap taunted me with promises of solace. But I stayed where I was, and cried. In the morning, when I opened my eyes, the hot residue was gone. The bed for summer visits spoke with relief as my foster mother sat up, fully clothed, and looked at me.

Dry, I felt no pain as I watched dense balls of fluff fall to the floor and my foster friend, brother really, sweep them up, eager to be involved. He'd experienced a few cuts but now his head's covered in scabs, suppressed hair, cultural significance dried up, so every time someone was getting a trim, there he'd be, broom in hand waiting for the 4C weeds to tumble to the floor. I once watched him put my hair in his pocket and inhale it behind a door. My scalp had some sores too, but the plump tangle of my hair kept it a secret my 1A carers had no reason to wonder about. When the cut was over and I slid off the chair, immediately forgetting my fro, there were no puffs of hair to cushion my steps, the job of sweeping them away done so well. I felt lucky only to get the snip because I'd seen the fits of the suffering girls – soft hair falling like floss, no fro to swell – white hands going into black hair but never acknowledging its curls.

I've never smiled again like I did on my sixth birthday, looking into the camera while my foster mother guides my hand through a symbolic slashing of years. I can feel the failing elasticity in her hand and smell the dissolving lungs on her breath. My foster dad, a quiet favourite, dozes, tired from a job I've never known him to have. Some kids are only here for summer. I watch them, unconsciously thumbing my singed skin, a scar from separated kin, a melding with warmth severed too late, and remember what loss feels like, deciding to stay around faces awaiting the same school as I am. I've crunched through several chocolate cornflake cakes before I remember I have presents to unwrap. I walk to the gifts, eager but satisfied, tonguing the soft cereal stuck to my teeth. I notice the handwriting on the first present and retreat to my foster mother's leg. 'All right, dear, we'll open this one later.'

He wasn't A's real dad or carer, so I struggle to place him in fostered thoughts. He liked sitting with his legs crossed in our living room eating cheese sandwiches. His posture, chewing and satisfaction made me envious, made me want to bite from the same plate he did, his full stomach moans enough to make me crave cheese in the extreme, casu marzu dripping and crawling through my dreams. She always asks for a piece and is refused and told to go get ready. Both gone, my mum preoccupied with plucking pheasant, I'd eat the crusts left on his saucer, which often had teeth-marked slices of cheese between them. A day came when I was able to open the fridge and take out the cheese, which first refused my knife, knowing the rules of the house, take two pieces of bread and create what was slowly becoming a delicacy. I took a bite and the static in my jaw shuddered through my body. I bent over the bin and spat out what I had desperately sought, realising getting what you want is not what you thought.

Thin lips beneath a film of moisture, my foster mother trying to teach me how to pronounce letters of the alphabet. We flip through *Biff and Chip*, me waiting for parts with Wilma.

Turning keys was fascinating to me so I clutch one and stroll off like a schoolboy, leaving the house searching for hours to help the bathroom door speak once more. I join the family but, bored, place my hands in my pockets and feel something cold and hard – I must own it. I step towards the table where my foster mother sits, regal, smoking while the sound of her children opening and closing doors, pacing around and climbing bunk beds combines with her nicotine to heighten effects dulled by chain smoking. I took the key, I confess, and expect a cane but am freed and taught the importance of honesty.

Cursive presents as the RP of pen to paper; I envy that dexterity denied me, the first difference of ability I noticed between myself and others. My foster mum finds pages of failed attempts, notes of a voice failing speech therapy, pain, straining imprinting on paper. She forces me to look at my writing, pointing at sentence after sentence, her finger finally resting on a tear absorbed, covering my shame, and then tells me my handwriting is lovely without the fancy lines.

My seatbelted body rose with the bumps, and with each bump dinner for the following days was decided. Pheasant, like rabbit, was delicious more than cute, and the smell of farmlands and my fascination as we drove by meant only chicken, pork and beef was barbaric. Tea time followed dinner time, the table spread with home-made marmalade and jam. Berries I picked myself, in between intervals of wiping up behind me with what I hoped would not sting. Blackberries were the easiest to find, evident from the black stains on my teeth, my foster mother becoming Ghanaian for a second in asking why I was acting like I didn't have anything to eat. There were blocks of jelly I dreamed of sinking my teeth into, unprepared but still as appetising as the bars of chocolate destined to be melted and mixed with a collection of cornflakes and spooned into paper casing – my birthday was approaching. On days that our village was tearful for my loneliness, I wore wellingtons and jumped in puddles imaging the same miracle that touched the delightful wardrobe. The air smelled like horses nowhere in sight, until we'd take a trip in the van and someone would scream, pointing to the first black beauty they'd ever seen. Trees were planted on my arrival but as I left, petitions were passed around. This countryside melody played so loud it was years before the sound of boots on mud and friendly good mornings was taken over by sirens and the smell of booze and latex, a door buzzing instead of knocked, faces that were not hostile but indifferent.

What does a persistent cough mean to a young boy who is sick? He thought it brought them closer, always together but holding onto words that never rose beyond the swirling smoke that stained the ceiling, a burning kept inside. He never said 'I love you' because he sat with her when no one else would, watched TV and listened to the browned floating leaves in her breathing, trickling down her throat, and tried his best during the darkest moments to see their reflection in whatever was screening. Her feelings meant a lot to him, so when feet scratched and scuffed the floor, children escaping to play outdoors, he stayed, and listened to her finish the sentence she had started. His love was listening, hearing her weak voice address an empty house, punctuated by unexpected, persistent coughs that would make any eye water, never believing that the day he left was the day the countryside sky would call her. Too naïve to know that with every inhale the cerulean summit drew close, and her halo glow meant smoke was signalling her home. If only he had known it was cancer revealing her bones. If only he had known that it was the offspring of smoke that brought her to tears, not her being happy her son was so near. His visits to London lengthened as tumour and organs grew fonder. I miss keeping you company after our dinners, I wish you could have stayed a little bit longer.

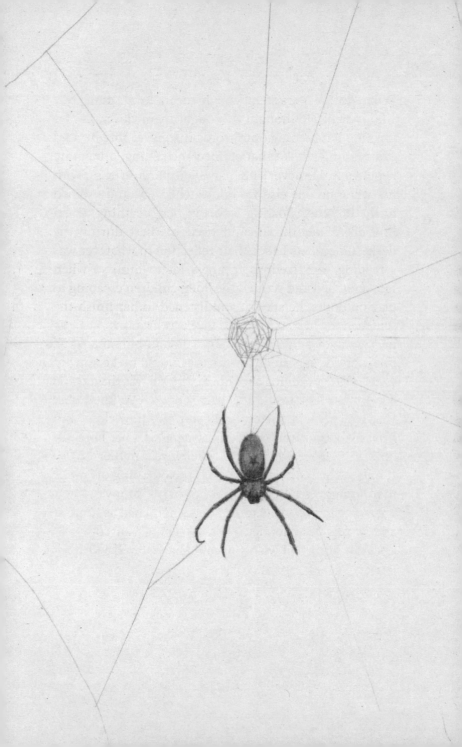

REFLECTION

Anansi, though we are similar, you are selfish with stories and I share mine freely. I rapped on your door with unwrapped tales, tying nothing up as Nyame intended, but still your father ignores me. I will touch the threads of your web once more and ask that you pass on my words to the sky we both adore.

My aunt's floor became a blow-up bed we sank into every night and hoped to rise above, where I'd dream about the hard surface I had come from. No heels hit pavement in my morning ear but I couldn't tell the difference. I didn't know we were poor because the preserves on savoury hors d'oeuvres, Jacob's, were so satisfying I could stomach at least twelve every time, scrambling to eat my own crumbs. I was happy to share my mother's hair-rollers, presenting as the girl she always wanted – but truthfully, they were fashion for her but soldiers for me. I'd pull up the clip part and bend it over the roll, arms ready for war, green vs pink, with my remotes on standby ready to change it all, silent, watching the brawl. Tottenham was beyond our balcony and every football match I'd hear the crowd shout for me, though I would turn my back, uninterested. We held onto superstitions tight as our silver; a few coins gathered to mix the farina with the mash. But often, the dry rivulets on my cheeks invited pound coins and 50 pence pieces from strangers that I'd have to throw away as soon as I got off the bus, a nervous flick of my hand as the disguise: to be generous was suspicious to the religious. A cultural fusion but paradox of Christianity.

I waited for friends while my mum waited for him. Our door was on the ninth floor but I was sure acquaintances would float through our window before my mum felt the gentle, now impatient press of the foreign body she once had. And she knew it, so she cried. But not the same tears for tongues that were brought forth for Christ – as long as I've got my god, K, everything's alright. In these moments, moments when James Avery, ready for an embrace, would flash before my eyes, all I could think about was my friend who had lied – with words so sure, he restored a shadow, one that only *seemed* to be looking over me – and told me that every person had a dad; this was compounded by the lie that you can't miss something you've never had.

My mum and I, we stand at a stop, the same one she said my dad had almost been picked up from, with his tight jeans and Rick James sex appeal that I wished he'd passed on to me, and, coincidently, where she believed an angel told her the world isn't hers to worry about. I have my hands around her thick coat, trying my best to steal some warmth, a more material form of affection that she can't hold back from me. But I am wrong. She pushes me away and I notice her breath in the cold air, a horizontal stream fading as it ascends, in imitation of a smoker's, so I focus on that, remembering another mum and trying not to feel the scorch of her scorn: I'm forced to feel warm. The bus arrives after five minutes and while I'm sitting, I'm offered another pound coin, one I imagine making a sharp sound on the icy floor when I'm forced to throw it away.

My first day of school a boy in year 6 asks me if I'm a rude boy. I'm not rude, I think, and carry on watching the girls playing marbles, waiting for the right moment to ask if I can join. I have a cat's eye but they ask how I can see through my dark skin.

On the second day the only student who will talk to me tells me to undo my shirt's top button, roll up my sleeves and walk with a bop. There's no official school uniform but second-hand shirts and trousers are cheaper than tracksuits so I always look smart and ready to learn and this, the boy informs me, makes me a bod. The transformation helps.

On the third day a girl in year 6 takes me round a corner, cups my face and kisses me. Her lips are soft and as they press against mine it feels like nectar from the pressure is trickling down my chin to branch out inside my chest and suddenly, I love London best. After a few weeks, my classmates are less hesitant to talk to me and soon even my teacher can address me without smirking at my clothes, my clogged shoes or my constantly split bottom lip. I'm told my breath smells like an African. I take the insult with baptised eyes, seeing who I am, unable to rebut it because as I lift my hand to cup my mouth, I can smell last night's soup still on my fingertips. It's past lunchtime so I lick them clean, unsure if I'm trying to savour the taste to subdue my speaking stomach, unsatisfied with the ham sandwich packed for lunch, or I'm embarrassed, revealed to be an African who eats with his hands. Some days I try to play football but I've never been picked because I do something called toe-punt, so I sit behind the goal and dig a stick into the grass, trying to create a grave for the ants that pass by. Maybe I'll join their march. I'm still in love with the girl in year 6. A teacher caught us pressed together behind a skip and I haven't seen the girl again. I'm in year 3. So now I just play with my sticks, watch the boys running after the football and think about the next person who'll want to be my friend.

3

The Color Purple. I sat so close to the TV I could hear the static, felt it shuffling around the down on my face. My hands were tightly grasping the covers; I imagined my grip had turned yellow sheets white, mirroring my desire for the fight for breath and bloody choking of Mister. I watched as, fresh from stroking leather, the blade hung in the air stealing kisses from his Adam's apple. With his head back, Celie moved in close to carve out control while he waits for the first stroke – the blade moist, beads of sweat, fear, instruments even nervous in his presence; the lather, complicit, exposed his skin so all it took was to ignore personal morality and hold your breath as the turpitude took over, cutting open what helped keep his head high. I sat on the edge of my bed, a bed moved into the living room where robed men sitting for supper watched sand surface in our eyes. My mum was asleep beside me, grinding her teeth as Celie was caught from behind, pulled out of a dream and made to walk back into a nightmare. I fell asleep without seeing it through to the end but for days after would depict Mister's death with my pen – a dark blue mood, purple was pain, bruised and beaten. Suddenly, it wasn't just my suffering confined to my pad; I wrote Celie out of her story and added her to mine, with the last drops of my ink gave us both a father neither of us had.

4

My aunt's feet beat the road, catching us just before we boarded a bus, handing over a different videotape: that's *The Golden Child*, she said, this is *Coming to America*.

Relieved that my interest settled beyond seeing the inside of electronics, my mum lets me sit in front of the TV rewinding and playing the first movie she saw me pay attention to. References to clean dicks and cartoon breasts with no sense of gravity streamed by as I waited for the end of the film, watching Eddie Murphy marry his Queen. He was Eddie to me because I believed the video was playing back something I couldn't remember, something that kept me quietly thinking when I wasn't rewinding to see the Prince remove the cover of his rosy-lipped Sunrise. Love speaks on, while sex needs time to breathe, and it was the echo of someone who loved me that kept me from thinking I needed to get a word in on my destiny. Feelings uninterrupted, I rewind the videotape one more time.

5

At first, sex was something the naughty wrote on the whiteboard, a word with consequences but not one with curious whispers that piqued my interest, opened me up to hardening images every few seconds. What caused me grief at night, left me running to the bathroom, two fingers squeezing the tip, trying not to soil my briefs, knew of sexuality only through fighting with a friend, both refusing to disarm. My cousin returned to the stairs from the living room, and I saw through the half open door his mum smiling, leaning satisfied against the closet, watching the glowing box that had inspired her to share secrets. My cousin spoke, each word building on the other, raising my disquiet. 'That's what a condom is; my mum just told me.' I watched as he became a man, retelling a secret lasting only a few seconds, while mine would never reach my lips. I believed what my cousin had said, knowing my friend and I could never really have sex. Sadness dropped my guard, and the next day I began to slow down when the girls would chase me for kisses.

6

My mum watches me bite the skin on the inside of my lip, places her palm on my hand and lowers my fist. Listen to me, K, the world is not yours. Her words open up into a bus stop on Tottenham High Road. My mum looks up the road, weavon protected by a Kwik Save bag, trying to will the digits that can open doors to get her home. Her nail polish is cracked, splintered first by her work and then by her nerves – floors are clean but her krata is still a dream. Beside her is a path that leads anywhere the foreign may choose, and peering into the area stripped of light, a silhouette, an outline where no rain seems to fall. Out walks a figure, dry, catching no one's eye but hers. They lower their hand onto her curved fingers, cold, but the chill creates warmth, moving them away from her mouth as she spits the last bits of varnish from her lips. 'Who does the world belong to?' they ask. 'Not you. So why do you worry?' These are closing words, nothing more is said – K, you think I saw them again? My tongue circles the inside of my mouth, tasting the metallic of the bitten sores, and the pressure of my jaw eases. This is her favourite story. I don't see her leave, my mum, having passed those words to me, again.

In the same hall where all nights murmured with prayers and bargains to God, I stand against a wall, looking on at all the colours and adinkra patterns that embellish the robes my aunties and uncles wear. The music imbibed shakes ancestors alive and permits only one dance; a side-to-side shimmy, causing partners to slowly eddy. My uncles become aunts and aunts uncles, bodies representing a language where gender has no use. She watches me, my mum, with a gesture saying, 'Come' – bottom lip upturned, eyebrows raised, hands swaying by her sides and an apology in her eyes. We've fought today but here, in the hall where prayers still linger, white handkerchiefs in the air waving them away, and Lumba's voice causes waists to limber, she looks like mother, her ntuma printed with akoma ntoso, my body understanding where my tongue can't reach, giving in to the cloth's impression. I approach, my steps wanting to forgive; our bodies get close, not one of us is speaking, no one is resisting, the music becomes a whisper as our dancing speaks and listens.

8

Our flat contained thoughts of God, my dad and Daniel O'Donnell. Country music called my mum while the homeland had a Western hand to keep its culture quiet, its palm giving off the odour of a corroded shovel and dirt. Irish accents and Twi became interchangeable during a sign-obsessed period of British life, and 'Give a Little Love' became more a clutch for capital, a tune dying before most could hear. My mum danced, – rhythmic with moves beyond the confining Ashanti shuffle – sliding on a tape worn out by thousands of steps, a tape that refused to give up while my mum swayed to its cassette. I sat by the player, watching, in love with the fusion of mother and music, my finger raised, ready to take it all back, keeping everything in time, or possibly pause a moment where there was no *other* life to define. Musical notations fell to splash in leaked puddles, the poverty of home became music with Daniel O'Donnell. My mum called his face the only mirror of virtue, that he sang words like it could never be in their nature to hurt you.

I hear the bouncing pitch of my mum's voice. 'That's how I talk', her defensive phrase, but her strain to bring forth 'English English', muffled by her Ghanaian accent suffocating every word, tells me something different, so I get up to check who she's talking to. She needs me. My dad is around, back on our sofa for another abbreviated visit, but will not help, dreams of East Legon keeping his eyes closed. I take the phone and speak in a stream of consciousness – sax-playing words and long-winded sentences I feel will move things into place. I set a date for the council visit and hand the phone back. I don't return to my room, I stand to listen to the end of the conversation – my mum able to say goodbye politely – to see all that I'd done, arms folded, satisfied. My mum hangs up, thanks me and squats on the floor to carry on mixing her pepper with double-sided pestle grinding the mortar. I watch her. Then I shout, 'Meeko dah'. She doesn't look up, only says, 'Okay, okay', the words nkwan to swallow her laugh.

There's no limit to my new family. New aunties and uncles are met every day. What was supposed to be my mum and I popping in to say hello becomes, by the end, concern that we'd missed our last bus home. Between the beginning and end of one back-and-forth homily, I look out of the window, down at the kids screaming (no way to tell who the sounds come from) and running around the small park between the flats, battling in the playground at its centre, jumping off the swings and balancing on the seesaw. And also, what I most want to do, standing close to the older boys talking.

I need to know what is said. I walk through the words of the family, unlatch the door and run along the corridor, down the stairs and out into the sun cooking my company of cousins, everyone Ghanaian. Slowly, I move closer to where the older boys stand and lean against the railings, a bar slipping between my bum cheeks. I realise they are not speaking English; they are speaking (what I know as) Ghana language. Aren't they embarrassed? Their bodies – chests in the air, rising with each response, or the breath of what they are smoking – speak as loud as their voices. One is connecting sentences with more frequency than the rest. He is telling a story. Here – Broadwater Farm, where any parked car could be police, where killers wipe off their fishing knifes before saying, 'hello, Auntie' – being Ghanaian is turning into something else. I listen, not understanding much, but feeling like somewhere in my chest I was hearing everything. Then silence, all of the boys look around at each other, a prelude to a burst of words: 'Wo boa!' 'heh, fa wa sɛm ko ɔuwhaa.', 'hwe lies na wo ka!' 'Don't mind him.' 'Ay, busy busy Griot. Griot of the estate. Tell some more, let us enjoy.'

Who was lying? I was hearing African pride and I was hearing the truth. And then a hand on my neck, pulling me back towards the flat. My uncle had seen me out of the window while smoking a cigarette, one sin revealing another, my aunt would say. But he was too late. I already I wanted to hear more from the Griot; I wanted to tell my stories too.

The Glory of God rests on Sundays so voices of praise have room to uplift. Gospel becomes the voice of God so Esther Smith sang salvation through a single breath of our Saviour. These mornings still held the sound of my mum fighting through tears, her fists in motion treating Satan as a speedball with an Azumah Nelson-like endurance before falling asleep. When sent to bath, my champion's pour was really a Goliath's gulp, with clean water splashing at my ankles as it was drained. I stepped out of the bathroom and my mum recognised that only tongues could cleanse the last of her litter. She pocketed anointing oil and I swallowed Seven Seas, even more hesitant these days since I split one open and the unbearable smell became the first time I questioned the odour of holiness. Sometimes my friends would already be out as I trailed my mum to the bus stop. Nodding at me, hoping one day I'd join them on these hot days. My mum grabbed my wrist and pulled me along. They knew better than to knock for me but sometimes, knowing the time I'd get home, they sent 'hw was chuch' messages on MSN. But, as post-praise conversations filled our rented hall, I would receive them too late.

The flat speaks its night noises and she responds with her own absent-minded murmurings. The kettle bubbles and the rising boil sounds and brings to mind the waters of Accra, Ghana, a memory of something she never experienced. When will she go back and stand before the tide she imagined as a child, waters that ignore boundaries and smother sands that eventually lead back to skyscrapers, distant from her and imagined – the Ghanaian garden city of Kumasi too traditional for a young mind tuned to Western standards of living. The tea is too hot but she's acclimatised, feeling only a familiar sensation, forgetting to register it as pain. It's 4.30, the bus comes in two minutes, but she'd rather be late than risk toppling over – no one would help her up in the morning mist or the lights of her own home. The school in which she works is quiet. You'd never know children ran up and down these corridors, so attentive is she to the floor, like wiping food from her child's face, showing it a gentleness she's always given but never received. Gospel hums in her throat, the words never coming for fear a teacher might pass and think her unfit for work. It's been twenty years and she's weary, the early morning wind feeling like a breeze visiting the edge of a cliff. Her humming is in sync with her thoughts, cleaning shit from toilets transforms into arms raised to the sky, praising at the feet of an almighty God – through everything, there sits her Saviour. She's finished by 7.30 and as she walks out of the building a teacher says, 'Hello, on your way?' She smiles, no words, her gentle hum is enough to think all is okay.

Its mouth spoke with small squeaks like a sound bubble popping with a weak peep and I saw it from a distance the dimensions of my room shouldn't allow. No sparrow had swooped in, stepped in stately with sandy feet, so I was sure what I saw came from wherever deities defined as outdoors. No face but I was aware of one, covered by the blurred wall between realities it seemed to have pushed its beak through. It was motionless for hours, still, blinks infrequent, but I was sure every time I closed my eyes that it drew closer but kept the same distance. It followed me from country care to a city where lights should have obscured its instruments, polluted its watching eyes by the lamps that force us to look for sparkles in the sea. One early night, where sapphire patches surrounded the colour of coals forging in the sky, it returned to me, appearing in my room with its mouth working out of time with the frequency of its peeps – and a bush brow now visible to show the range of its furrows. It was incensed by my leaving and not saying a word. But it's always been this way, my words unable to leave my mouth as the thing's own played the high-pitched sound of my imagination. That was the last night I saw it. At daybreak, as I lifted myself onto my elbow and my lashes fluttered away my fancies, I saw a mousetrap covered in peanut butter and its victim's mouth closed.

The first friend I allowed in my house ran back to tell our class I was poor. They saw my mum and dad's mattress lying on the uncarpeted floor – homeless, unsupported, the framework having fallen apart, with sheets seeming to drag along like a dropped flag gliding through an ocean of scattered clothes. When we bickered in school, my living conditions were his weapon of choice. Although the house didn't smell of spice, curry powder or Maggi, the white boys of the area instead mocked the visible tinge of black that stained the bottom of our inner curtains. They were there when we moved in and I suspect it was this unwillingness to change them, maintained by financial difficulties, that led the old woman from five doors down to knock at ours and enquire about her friend. In our garden we had a bomb shelter, fascinating to me but really a reminder of how soon the house might crumble. Suitcases longing for their promised flight to Ghana waited patiently next to Lidl bags full of sardines that kept guests company in our living room, distracting them from the black mould that gathered in the corners of our ceiling. Still, nobody left our home without a story of relative poverty to relay – the truth is, we were all black working class, but pretending we couldn't relate.

My dark skin saved my dad from child services but no one saved me. My mum's eyes were always elsewhere, too out of reach to pull me into something akin to sympathy. Her eyes were dry as they fell to the floor – fingers down a neglected window, down my childhood photos, the ones taken by door-to-door photographers, a blue background I now see as a sea I could mercifully push my younger self into. Connecting slaps, like feints and jabs, worked up his confidence, more coming as if encouraged by an imagined applause. Confusion had left me, leaving only lies I'd tell myself about who I was: I must be a bad boy; I must deserve it; I must have done something wrong; the knocks on my head a father's premonition? My dad, he walked with his head low, hands in pockets, not even seeing the pavement, and I wondered what he thought about, aside from the punitive ways to communicate with me. One evening I followed him out, with my head still in the itchy state of pain that followed his knuckles – as I walked and watched, stepping on the long shadow he cast, I thought he'd stroll out into the road, so unseeing he looked, so uncaring. Trees behind houses swayed with the wind, like giants in the darkness peeking round homes to see if he was okay. I felt sympathy – I watched him cross the road and enter the shop, but ran home when I saw him making his way back. Walking into the living room, he looked down at me; my peripherals filled with his presence, I kept my focus on the screen, on Kenan, Kel and Coolio. He threw something into my lap as the last nick of the show's theme tune echoed out – a bar of chocolate, a peace offering or manipulation disguised as guilt. I began to eat it, broke off a piece and offered it to him – but he spat back, 'I bought it for you; and make sure you eat it all.'

The pirate film we were watching mirrored my half posture among these white bodies sitting tall. The opening scene begins with singing and stretched arms anticipating the embrace of the good life. Then, the spectacle – the white upper class – father, rector, whatever, on the keys – enunciating every word of a rap written to help shake people like them off. Drum machines and keyboards are replaced by the more civilised piano, and voices full of money sing in unison the coarse lyrics smoothed over by their gentle diction and intonations. The black nerd is replaced by white intellectuals, keys on the piano unlocking racism I never knew existed. We were at a friend's house and his dad, hands worked to black by the grease of his motors, sat with us, a break from the MOTs and overcharging OAPs complaining of cataracts and not carburettors. The opening scene continues with Pharrell's chorus being sung by members of a church known for exorcisms and civilising missions in Africa. A line is said, removed from irony because of past pale hands tightening a noose – the Wayans brothers too unsophisticated to realise this truth. The dad among us laughed, licked his brandished teeth, satisfied on his break without having something to eat. I saw his pupil in the corner of his eye, so strained it nearly spilled out like mascara. He called me a nigger without opening his mouth. The movie played on and I wondered what was said when I wasn't sitting in this house.

How much pride did she feel removing my belt with one hand, seeing my jeans drop like trite comedy, an erection on the way but blood not knowing exactly what to do. I couldn't take my eyes off the cracked plaster, where a mirror used to be, as she rubbed and squeezed, kept her knickers on but tried to remove my boxers while I forced my body up against the wall. I wanted her, but not this, and as the kids ran past the bathroom giggling and looking through the keyhole, an older voice moving them on, there grew less of me for her to hold in her hand. But we rubbed on until I opened my eyes, both of us now sitting at the top of the stairs, in love and enjoying the view. She drew red crayon on her lips and asked me to be her boyfriend. Between kisses, I looked around for my belt – my mum can't know I've lost anything today. But I didn't want to pull away, and soon, I forgot. Of the girl, the last I remember is my mum asking me who she was between strikes from the belt that was to replace the one I had lost.

CHANGE

Anansi, the weight of the world can never fall on the sky, so this is why your father has no empathy for me. Does he sleep to my stories or are you weaving words without care? Creep to his bedside and wake him with these pleas, and I'll wait for the raindrop that proves his sympathy.

The distance behind us pulled itself into shapes in motion – something trying to be free and the night exposing something troublesome. The four of us stopped as the pacing got closer, the urgency in the stride frequency preparing us for a loss. 'Phones, phones.' My white friends pulled out their 3210s and Nokia face-offs while I felt in my pocket thinking I could assemble a cellular on a cellular level, use shaking fingers, the feelers drawing attention to the coins in my pocket, to bend reality. In this moment I was the shelves I had stolen from and the purses I had pillaged, justified, I thought, because it was unfair others had things and my material wants endlessly sought satisfaction. 'You're safe, you don't need to worry.' They said it like I should know better, like they were tired of explaining this. Slowly, they headed back into the half light that housed them. The four of us continued on our walk home, them feeling naked and robbed, not because of their loss but because I was safe. 'Bad boys' weren't just mindless men morphed from the darkness, but people like me. I looked at my friends and for the first time I felt a power I was sure they could see – I was no longer worried they would leave, now there were others just like me.

I watch a little black boy standing outside a shop, pre-tending not to be bothered by his white friends inside spending money. I walk over and give him a two pound coin and remind him to eat whatever he buys before he gets home. My mum wouldn't approve so I know his mum wouldn't either. Wide, his eyes look like mine and I fall in love with how grateful everything about him becomes. 'Safe, man!', he says. He smells like cocoa but-ter and DAX and I follow his scent up to the door and watch as he stands in front of the colourful sugars with snappy names. I know he's savouring being spoilt for choice; I'm sure when he takes a bite of whatever he buys I too will be satisfied. And a memory comes back to me of the first time I held a pound coin, given to me by a stranger who smelled like cigarettes and Blue Magic.

My mum carried around the ultrasound now come to life – an image swollen with my future – to show me nothing's black and white. I imagined a fragile sticker on her stretch-marked stomach and always walked behind her as she climbed the stairs. We'd fall asleep together, me supposed to be watching over her but getting caught up in the lethargy of her movements. I would wake before her and lift the kente from her stomach, the cloth getting acquainted with who it'd hold up, and imagine the smile of my soon-to-be sibling. And as I'd fall back to sleep I'd ask the bump for their name and glide my fingers over stretches and paths, trails to a world and a body's resistance to the light. Dribbling in the womb became spittle in a bucket, only my hands touched it, and pouring it out was simply wiping the baby's mouth. When my father walked out, I walked in, with a Cornetto in one hand and my pocket smelling of Deep Heat. Then my mum grabbed my hand so I could feel the kicks, but as I touched her stomach I knew it was a palm trying to connect with me through the skin, and my bond with my brother touchingly began.

She says she can't get up, that my dad looked down at her and walked away, his steps silent, like a stranger, like no one, only hissing sounds between his lips as he sucked the evening's meat from his teeth – just another day. Her hand is on her hip, a position she's used to, dancing alone to a beat she doesn't own. My bedroom door is open so she crawls across the floor, metamorphosis to tɛfrɛ my father has chosen to ignore. She reaches out, one hand on the bed frame, weak, but it shakes, trembling like it fears it'll have to cover where she lay. But she reassures it with a second hand and slowly, she stands.

A ward like this gave me my brother, memories where I could see life contributing to every colour, but today the sedate shuffling of nurses is different, lacking, less, there are no hearts left, and what was once a fast beat is now slow feet dragging with grief. I hear no babies crying but whimpers of a soul worn out – the hospital holds no excitement; who am I holding this time? My mum, she's too weak to hold her head. I lean over and let her hear the heart she brought forth to beat out her sadness, a child soaking it all up. She cries like gentle hiccups, trying to open her mouth to speak; I lift her to see her cheek and give it a kiss intended for two – Mum, I'm sure she would have loved you as much as we do.

I'm on first-name terms with my dad, the man my mum says should be on my birth certificate. I see him sometimes, usually once he returns from Accra, business trips that require Primark gifts and six months' saved salary – this mouse-like miser of a man would suddenly open up, speaking and giving enthusiastically when a runway crossed his mind. I've been building the courage for years, trying to pull my voice from a well that deepened with every strike, intimidated by the width of his arm when he wore traditional garb. As a child, I wished the colours of his kente would soak into him and give me a father whose personality was luminous; instead he'd pass on darkness to my eyes. But now I have the courage, just enough strength to go against the awkward, ominous silence that will follow my questions. A few years ago, I would have shielded my face hearing a feather float – a silence spoke of violence, an oncoming slap or a fist, a release to appease a broken heart for a life that God didn't give. I ask why he didn't show us any love, behave like the fathers who teased me as a child. 'K, I'm incapable,' he says. His head is low and I can see he is balding and for the first time his Ghanaian humility betrays his Nigerian features. 'My dad, you don't know,' he says, 'when he used to see me on the market he would ignore me. I don't know.' And for a moment I'm soft enough to let the weight of his confession mould me, leave an impression I'd carry round with me from now until the end. But then, I remember, years ago, a man's voice from our bathroom telling someone on the phone he loves them. My mum was asleep upstairs and the next day was my dad's fourth trip of the year to Ghana.

The hospital visits were every six months. Time off school isn't as fulfilling when you can't blink without pain, move your hand or cough without feeling the pressure of living. Tests showed no allergies but my dad returning stopped the symptoms that started with his departure. His presence felt oppressive but without him my body reacted the way I wouldn't allow my emotions to. On regular days, I'd greet him and take his groans or yeahs: but returning salutes, akwaaba, revealed a truth: a, 'How are you?' or 'You takin' it easy?' Was a panacea brought back from his home.

He'd had enough practice – you could tell by the dark stains on the tops of his shoes. I wouldn't let him get used to dragging his feet, so I lifted him out of his stroller, pushed him up overhead, his soles gliding back and forth faintly above my shoulders, giving him a taste of what it felt like to be above me: he has to be, my saviour – my reason for living. He baptised me, saliva on the top of my head like syrup spreading across my thoughts, my brother so lovable. He came forward, swaying, or maybe the floor shaking but in the moment I couldn't tell, so focused on the miracle of teaching that anything else seemed possible. He stood a few centimetres in front of me, one foot forward, his left, but I'd seen him beat his bowl of baby food with his right. He remained in that position, his torso teetering, a boxer learning to stay in the fight. Our local shopkeeper called him Tyson, my brother, big for his age and his chubby balled fist resembling a baby boxing glove. But here before me, his hands were open, stretched out in front of him because he wanted to be picked up and lay his head beside my neck. But, as I had, he would have to work for affection, nothing would come to him. He brought his left leg back and started again with his right. My smile at his discovery excited him and added to his unbalanced shaking, the unsteady jittering of laughter and weak legs. His left foot followed, and then another step; and then another, and another. 'P, you're doing it!' His joy from the journey nearly toppled him before he fell into my arms, Mike into D'Amato, a victory for us both.

A boat party on the Thames is the first time Miss Harry speaks to me. There was purposeful avoidance in the way she walked around me in class, collecting other students' work with small talk but acting in a daze when she lifted my sheets. During an assembly where she sank too comfortably into her seat, she rose to reveal a pink thong above her curve-concealing trousers. The laughter, I thought, was forced, to dissolve the embarrassment. But me, I didn't laugh. I just looked at her and she looked back. Now I'm leaning over the sea, watching its foaming, soapy so fish stay fresh, reflecting the corner of the sky where the moon is bubble-wrapped in darkness to protect it from poets. Miss Harry walks over and asks why I'm out here alone, and I answer with the truth, that I was hoping sympathy would compel feet heading for another dance to walk out into the fresh air and let me dream I had a chance. Miss Harry says anyone would be lucky. My left arm goes numb; she's staring at me to see what she's done. Thank you, Miss, I say. I bring back structure, the scaffolding of the school, the respect in my posture. She looks over the edge of the boat, focusing on the split in the sea, thinking it must be satisfaction these dark bodies of water receive. A smile and she walks away, a secret pressed tightly within her gait. Once out of sight I turn back to the distance, the wind whistles with my pining, a soft sound above water, a symphony without rain, a heart pierced without pain.

Our bathroom was filled with bath soap instead of bars and shower gel, my mum being unable to tell the difference, so when I tried to masturbate for the first time, the right consistency was close to hand. For a few seconds I rubbed and expected the suds to create a sensation that would turn me into a man. At fifteen, my cousins brushed beards between bringing out their dicks for banter, so I assumed maturity flourished because they were open to tags like Onan. Testosterone, I thought, must be forcing hair from follicles, and being versed in the use of a phallus made everything sexual well-balanced, uninteresting and only useful when ticks signalled moving hands or rare consensual pleasure. To them, a flaccid penis was nothing amorous until engaged. But now, at eighteen, my beard still fails to connect, and porn is a page I haven't turned yet.

I was spending the night – travel having succumbed to its own slumber in the open garage a walk away, numbers having their calculated rest. I heard the miss-measured door brush the carpet and toes testing the fabric-ated waters before bringing down the sole – and as he silently stepped into my room I knew what he wanted. Looking back, I could smell the salt of singed cities – our own reactions as children making us equally stiff – never penetrating the true nature of our embraces and delicate kisses but feeling comfortable with the romantic ripple in our stomachs. As a child, second hand words and sermons in Twi put me in my place so the spectrum of sexuality never moved me – a straight walk even if I could decide on a direction – but I loved him, remembered his unmoving body on mine not knowing what to do, remembering how impossible and never touching him again. Now, I offered him the shelter of my covers – praying for further remission as I pulled him closer to my face – his breathing anticipating something that could never happen – knowing by morning, comfortable in my linen, still he'd be reluctant to come out. His scent hadn't changed – Ashanti-brown cocoa butter inseparable from the smell of strawberry chewing gum on his breath – a few chews and he'd swallow, sweetness too intense to hold in his mouth, feelings he'd need to shout. I'd sleep and rise well if I kissed him – my best friend who could have been more. I slid my arm from under his neck to get up and quietly closed the bedroom door.

Once the satisfaction speaks to my entire body it becomes clear that not all sins are equal. As taught, I tie a knot in the latex opening, place the filled prophylactic in tissue and put it in my pocket. My hand hovers over the youthful receptacle while I hum songs of worship I was taught as a child, Ghanaian gospels I would clap to, trying to move my mother with my praise. God's jealousy of old flies through folds of time, forgiving my mum being deified but standing above, peering down like a parent who'll never be satisfied. Every night I've prayed the same prayer through compulsion and fear of the numinous; but tonight I'll fail to bring my palms together without regret at not having tried a different position. She had invited me in, put her hands on my shoulders and collapsed me into a chair. She moved the thin wrapper into her mouth like unleavened bread, prepared me then moved material to the side, lowering the experience of her sins on my thighs. And I sat on her tongue, Jonah 1:3, no longer able to spit out James 4:17 to save me from the judgement of my desires. The journey home, bus deserted, I hold the seat in front, a crash imminent, and with my hands secure I rest my head on my forearms, thinking back to when I'd pushed her thighs off my own, fearing I'd fall out of the chair as it groaned. And as I draw closer to my street and stare blankly at my phone, a mirror blazing, I feel the heat of hell unmistakably my own.

I found porn between my dad's vinyl of Prince and Rick James. Its plastic casing reminded me of pirated games, cheating companies. I was disgusted, bypassing arousal because I've never known sex – the pressure, the pulsing, the sweat and post revulsion. But I've felt close, and that's what I want. I daydream of dissolving, reaching for you to join my dissolution. Our skin touching, I imagine we become who we'd like ourselves to be. But we're blocked, never really touching, scientifically speaking, and look absurd while we're fucking. I've said I'd rather not, not tonight, but I know the mood swing will end in a fight – manipulation, out of sight. So I give in, am taken in, a smooth swallow, then rapturous applause, building, only to plummet to slow palms, a sarcastic clap – a peak nearly reached; I climb the crescendo one more time, I feel like I'm going to die, shrieks and scratches on my chest, shouts to go deeper, having nothing left. So out of breath, so out of my zone, and as I climax I'm dreaming of being home. And then we're done, both bereft, smouldering without satisfaction, a fire drained of air. Her bloodshot side-eye makes me want to run and hide. She needs a man and I'm a boy; she wants to make love and I want to be in love. I imagine myself small, knees up, my temples against my caps and my arms wrapped around them. Footsteps pass me and someone asks . . . but there's nothing wrong with me. I climb out of bed, pretending to scratch my pubic hair to conceal my flaccidity. I close the bathroom door. With my head in my hands, feeling my penis retreating, embarrassed by how we're leaving, I sit on the seat and cry.

I've been cosplaying with my clothes since earning the money to fill my wardrobe, starting with two three-piece suits hanging either side of the railing like large ornamental earrings on a face that doesn't need much dressing. Tracksuits were folded beneath tailored cuffs, the descent of man, with skinny jeans stacked next to those and a partnered pile of £3 muscle fits from Primark. All black. Jamal, Marcus, Del Boy, K, Nana – whatever day of the week a new name, look and stride would guide my inverted feet. But one thing has stayed the same since I started pushing my burden uphill everyday: my dark shades, dark shades that hide red eyes but can't cup falling tears. Feet firm in front of my mirror as the moon looks on and muses the same – wondering which one of me is standing before you today.

I am a regular at my brother's school. The sight of me always draws an embarrassed but proud smile across his face – older brothers emanate power but bring infancy into focus. We're watched as we walk out and I know tomorrow he'll be asked, for the tenth time, 'Is that guy your brother?' He's one step away from a sprint, struggling to keep pace with me as we walk home, neither of us talking but enjoying being seen together, me looking after him and him feeling like my equal. We're stepping into the house before he asks what's for dinner; he can smell the rice but wants to be wrong, I want to be wrong, the corned beef stew on my tongue becoming the taste of PERi-PERi chicken. 'Go and get changed and I'll dish your rice.' He takes his time then sits on the edge of the sofa, knees ready to hold the plate, tray and rice. I bring in the Nando's and again there's that smile, embarrassed but proud.

Outside the eyes of God there are no sins; I learned deceit
when I decided to give my life to Christ. Timid, with a
voice too weak to reach salvation, I was told to speak up
and be heard, bounce my words off the drums of God,
played by the young West African boy waiting for citi-
zenship but finding a home in church. My pastor – their
'Daddy' – told stories of sex, drugs, his first testimony,
matrimony, and, I'm sure, years later, his succumbing to
infidelity. Sins are stories given to Anansi to warn children at bedtime; a web of lies filled and taken over by the
locust invading from across the sea. What didn't touch
the brink of spiritual abuse was spoken of by gargling
deacons as sipping on the devil's juice. I rested on community centre seats as the horn of judgement bellowed
from the throat of our leader. And in feeling no rapture,
I knew it was over. I knew as I sat and soothed myself
with musical thoughts of consequences played out over
inherent value, that purple rain contained no trumpets.
I smiled as all heads bowed for the closing prayer, mine
containing only a thank you; I stood and turned my
back to the pulpit, attentive to the standing of goodness
without the worship of crucified statues.

I took bread out the freezer and heard the front door slamming, a sound then swallowed up by the half-banshee screams of my cousin, who, apparently, had barely survived: his pace had saved him from stumbling to the other side. He wanted something, anything; 'Where is it?' he asks, 'Hurry up and get the ting.' I put my hand inside the sandwich maker to gauge the heat. I'd been craving, roasting for toast bread and margarine since I woke up, since the smell of weed and soaked socks drying on the radiator took over from the oily stench of cockroaches. I had shaken a small one off my toothbrush and held it under the running tap, only for a few seconds, remembering we'd get billed for that, while my cousin, Ghanaian so not bonded by blood, told whoever was outside to suck their mum, yes, the day had now begun. I took my breakfast into the sitting room but stood to eat, my cousin not even noticing me watching him dig something out of the back garden grass, two of his friends on guard but blocking his path – how long will all this last? I took a bite of toast and felt the melted margarine between my teeth – a passage where the working class meet. My cousin found what he'd been looking for and I turned away, brushing crumbs off my vest, thinking about the Doppler effect, knowing I'd be hearing sirens next.

Act 1

The tapping gets louder the closer I get – I turn onto my cousin's street and the youngest, twelve, is beating magnetic tags against the concrete garden wall. He keeps a rhythm, a steady tempo, not quite 140 bpm but close, while he imagines wearing the Adidas tracksuit grime artists get for free – no one asks how any more, only where – he tells me JD, but he sold all the electronics as soon as he got them. Inside the house there's another trill but this time it's the high-pitched excitement in a voice still holding the strain of yesterday's cacophony, too much discord to be a revolutionary chant. I try to take a seat but no one moves, or looks, the narrative holding them hostage, my cousin carrying on with his story, finally getting the attention he's always wanted, embellishing each interesting detail with a hand gesture I need to dodge. You could film him and he wouldn't notice, a face that's photo ready – 'Where were you? – I went raving – No after party, though – Police locked it off – I tried to call you – Why, what happened?'

AMI is the new ting but north man don't do it, only south man do – I ask my brother what AMI stands for and he tells me he can't remember.

Our politician is standing in front of microphones held by pale fingers – he is condemning the young black boys who were building on past aggressions and revolutions, blindly, yes, but an encroaching state not unforeseen. There is a charred bus in the background and a Hasidic Jew walks past but the camera becomes unfocused.

At the end of a jog, I approach a melee in the street, my brother is bleeding from his brow and screaming for me to back it but I don't, I talk everyone out of their violence – my brother walks towards the house, still seething. I follow, there's blood dripping down his cheek, and when we arrive at the house he shuts the door in my face.

Girls are screaming and boys, black boys, are shouting – an arm shoots in and out of a side car window, like a quick morning effort to remove ice from a windscreen, the blade gleams, and noticing my fear my cousin asks, 'Have you never stabbed someone before?

Act 3

If you lined up TVs tuned to news channels, the flames would blow through the sets. No respite from the pings of broadcasting messages – BlackBerries finally used for the business of organisation – the age of spectacle has no limits, no finish applied to the awards handed out for partaking in the farce of revolution. But we saw the shortlist days afterwards, each face boxed in preparation for the body. Before the skies could rumble like the throttle of a god preparing to speak over what it foresaw as a London pulse starting to slow, I had saved twenty new numbers in my phone, people I recognised in the paper but hardly spoke to, someone had to, although the entire ends would probably see it for themselves soon. The day after the riots, I walked through the streets, wondering where the first bottle was thrown, and had the urge to repeat the action to believe I too had been initiated into history. Dreaming I'd fallen from the mind of Matheson, I carried on walking through the silent district, knowing the roads felt betrayed – dole money not paid so no smoke reached up, as if expelled from the appendix of modern houses, blown from bookie doorways – but the pavement still had ashes to sate its appetite, leftovers from last night's part piecemeal. Wandering around, I looked for signs of life and imagined the animated street was hiding in the only bus in sight, its black body tattooed by flames not enough to deter my imagination – they'll take that away too, I thought – and as my memory comes back from these moments, I'm grateful for the words: 'Where were you?'

Act 4

WE ARE THE POLICE. I felt like Orwell, Owen or Olson standing on the sideline and reporting, each update seconds apart, no profession persuading me, capturing everything – every bottle thrown, every car set alight, every female officer toppled by a miscalculated baton swing resulting in opportunistic Nikes attempting to stomp her out. I broadcast to another world, my Twitter feed my *Daily Planet*, the place to dump news like leftover thoughts. I was on the train home when the announcement of Hackney Downs reminded me of the London ember gaining air, the riots reaching disconnected regions making up the body of the news. I ran down the station stairs focused on the fray, taking backroads and sliding under police tape. But the scene took me back. I was my father in '85 seeing so many losing their heads. I stood watching videogame-obsessed teens trying to throw Molotovs but only managing Mojitos, a baby screaming above fire licking windows, trencherman flames eating up curtains, and a boy, maybe fourteen, bleeding from his shin because the excitement forced his foot through a glass window that didn't shatter but broke in half. I put my phone down, the novel I was threading suddenly revealing itself as true crime. I shook off the stupor, joined in with the screams to save the baby and began to help the boy.

Every evening my brother comes in racing the sun to twilight, I worry he has killed somebody. He says he is friends – boys – with everyone he knows, used to kick ball with them in farm, Clasford's livestock, when they were younger, so now they're safe and grown. But as tone-deaf ads were telling me, you need a five-a-side to know your enemy truly. I can't cover for you, P, I can't lie if feds knock: a truth hard to swallow when you were expecting comfort food, but I can't get my hands dirty even if I'm funding you. We're standing in our living room, our mum pretending to sleep on a sofa recently freed from plastic sheets, so she can move freely without our noticing but as she snores I'm sure she thinks we'll ignore her closed eyes' perceptible blink – what does she think? Confronted, my brother pulls the blade – a long reflection on its side that turns Tottenham into the Everglades   from inside his Adidas bottoms, the length of the weapon comfortable next to the branded lines, its handle level with his hips. 'So now you're Catcher Freeman?' He laughs, his wide mouth an invitation to talk him out of his journey. I take the tool from him and give him back his future; twenty-five years for the blade, but for the rest he'll need to hand me the gun.

The cut above my brother's eye is still healing the day he hears the news through his Xbox headset. 'So he's dead?' I ask. 'Yeah. Stabbed.' My brother is lying on the mattress in my mum's room playing FIFA online, gloating over a goal as if his past friendship still remained as his current rivalry, his on-sight relationship. I don't believe him. 'P, how do you feel about that? You two used to be friends.' 'I can't pause online games, bro. Talk to me later. But what goes around comes around, innit. Oh my days, man, that should've been a goal. See, you're distracting me.' I walk out, the final echo of a groan slipping through my door before I close it. They scored again. I lean up against my wall and stare at my curtains. I forgot to draw them this morning and I can see the light trying to push its way in, blocked but unsuccessfully contained by the weak cap of my curtains. I walk over and open them.

It sounds like an air ambulance descending to lift him to safety, but opening his eyes he sees the wheels of a skateboard stuttering along, dipping into thin gaps in the pavement. The police arrive to watch his watery eyes glitter like an ocean shining off a star, his closing statement, the suspect bleeding to death outside the open-till-late off-licence. Police seal off the road as the shopkeeper walks back into the light of his livelihood, shaking his head like he can tolerate only a few more deaths before he hands the shop over to his son, the son who now changes his clothes and wraps something in his T-shirt.

A mother does the washing, remembering to turn certain clothes inside out because he hates the effect of fading. She separates the socks and tosses a bio capsule into the washing machine, usually powder into the appliance's pocket but she's aware it sometimes leaves chalk-like streaks on his tracksuits. She watches it spin for a while. Then brushes a few fallen leaves with the inside of her foot, like passing them back to the trees, as she puts on her rubber gloves, mixes the liquid with the warm water and begins scrubbing him. He's a newborn once more, looking up at the face who's twice kept him alive, bathing him clean, presentable when people come to visit. She's on her hands and knees telling him about the latest drama in the family. He always listens. And that's all she needs. For her son to hear her voice and know he's still her baby.

The scene: hands hovered waiting for the mic, like pincer index and thumb ready for the draw. The odour is stale, a dull sheen on plaqued teeth has left moisture on the mic, ignored by the MCs anticipating their next hit. From outside, the estate pulses – the surging energy of the set has became the heart of the city – with splintered thinking, one half focused on embellishing their boys 16, 32, 64, long ting, while listening for the next drop, and the other half searching through the mental scattering of lyrics penned on A5 schoolbook pages that will flow well on the beat creeping in. As the next track drops, hands follow suit – it's not a riddem they can ride and hype to get casual listeners on their side. How many think about the broadcast and how many are just in the moment, oblivious to the structure they're building – Tetris blocks dropping with each bar, that background jingle a doppelgänger of the instrumental that fills the room. A blooming legend wipes sweat from his face, top to bottom, you can hear the flow, then carries on with his 140 bpm birdhead bop; another young face is looking upwards with eyes rolled back, possession palpable through the epileptic movement of body, mumbling what was written down yesterday evening in front of the eMachine only used for solitaire and Sixteens. The upload to LimeWire is complete before MCs have left the building, some on beef, wondering if that bar was about them, others absconding without paying subs. Some will be back tomorrow, new material, today's missed drop ethereal, ready to climb the steps and once again become the pacemakers of the capital.

I spot her on the train. I look up and squint as she rolls her suitcase over my toes – where was auntie behind those glazed marbles? Seventy, I think, with dark rings around her eyes and warts peppering the skin beneath, everlasting weeping, I say to myself. She sits down with an open-mouthed sigh, opposite me but one seat to the left. She's tired, but instead of leaning back she's resting her forearm on the top of her case, looking around curiously, but missing me, her eyes slipping over my dark skin. I'll get off at her stop, take my time behind because I know she'll take hers, sentimental about every second, a walk every seasoned West African aunt seems to have – almost limping, one foot in a grave no one is willing to dig. She hums 'Mawon San', she's hopeful, taking slow strides into what must be a Sunday. I focus, give myself time to think – I'll move around to her right before I reach, stop her going anywhere like footsteps in her sleep, the angle paying respect to cultural customs. We stop at the stairs and I step up and gently place my right hand on the handle of her suitcase. 'Let me help you, auntie,' I say. 'Thank you, son,' she says. I carry her luggage and stand with her on the escalators, watching her rest – Ma, you're doing your best. I leave her at the barriers, turn back with my own luggage and continue on my way home.

We sleep in the same bed long after I should have grown into my own. I kneel on the mattress cornering my mum, asking why she sent me away, why she allowed me to be raised by people whose lives were so different from our own, people she didn't even know. My side of the bed is still tender with my silhouette. My mum reaches over to my indent and tells me not to speak ill of the dead.

She trusted me to keep her alive, to deify, to render her an immortal that cancer couldn't metastasise. Thousands of stacked monitors going out one by one, a memory on each and then darkness to close the scene. Most of our loves die lying – dropping out of time, leaving broken promises behind. Mum, I thought you wanted to stay. But instead, when I turn back, I see, you were like me but you did it by smoking twenty a day. Why choose to die? I could have saved you, with my towel safety-pinned around my neck, a Boy Wonder wondering how to defeat the evil smoke monster rising to the ceiling. Lose a memory and you've lost a life – so hands stretch into the darkness to bring our living thoughts to the light. Shaking the limbic like a Polaroid until the image is clear, I stare at the face I think I remember, confused as to why you're not here. If I forgive your absence, then you have to forgive mine, forgive me for not showing up and for struggling to keep you alive. And though we're not in contact, you'll always be my mother; we'll meet again because we never said goodbye.

Loss is scratching the latex off a calling card and waiting for the delayed 'Ete sɛn' from a line reaching 4,000
miles into the past – across dictatorships, heads of abrofo
beneath the stool, rebellions before the porting of ships.
Loss is a reminder, when starved to reheat the assorted
meat soup from the day before, that the perpetually hun-
gry cheeks of the deceased clinging to the fridge door
will never feel the sting of pepper soup on bitten-down
nails, or nervously torn lips. Loss is the profile on the
bottle opener as you flip the cap of your malt – the skin
pulled tight on a face that never looked up into a colo-
nial sun; it's the tired eyes looking up from the napkin,
vision akin to ɔkra developed through midnight walks
from evening cleaning; it's the keyring that sounds hol-
low in conflict with pure elements, the key that starts the
engine, the body bursting with black and white ntoma,
the Nyame Mwu na Mawu symbol prominent, as another
funeral journey begins; it's the sticker on my living room
door, the cup from which I drink, within the surface of
the corn-beef-stew-stained plate languishing in the sink.
In our house, where Twi holds loss within each of its syl-
lables, we sing songs of thanks, remembering what we had.

Farina and mash whet my appetite for a taste of home, so for a third time I travel to find acceptance. Hostile humidity strikes me as I walk down the steps. I'm an exile recovering too late, too out of touch. Bag check(s) because the repatriate cedis are unwanted by every corrupt body in the airport. The drive to the coach station is absorbed by gloom; I alone take in the sights of runners hoping to pace their way into the Premiership, while my mum and auntie, anxious but focused, look for joggers too close to the car. I rise to crowing chickens unaware it's them who will be betrayed, guided into the garden of our compound where no god will stop the raised blade of Abraham; we call him Paa Kwesi. In the afternoon the sun beats down inspiration for the rhythmic descent of pestle onto mortar. I ask to be taught, beat my best imitation of culture, but a few motions in I'm told to hand back the instrument. I watch the plantain pounded into cassava, both having no choice but to mix, body kiss, a matrimony that will fill us up and welcome me home. My aunt turns the fufu skilfully in time with the beating, Chronos curving, her partner stops to shoot sweat from a finger while she rests, but we're soon presented with the meal, chicken now in pieces with yellowish fufu floating in the soup – aburofɔ aduane too, paling in comparison. I snip at the sticky swearing-in and my grandma, watching with a smile, says, 'Akwaaba!'

I've never stood above a grave but I have witnessed the birth of children.

We strolled through Asokwa streets, the smell a gift to nostalgia, sound beating on the silence, and saw a man sleeping in the dust, people stepping over him like his peace was too sweet to disturb. I asked my mum who he was and she referred to him as 'the body'.

I remember my brother was born on a Sunday. He came ceremoniously, purple with trauma and seemingly disturbed by the other cries taking up his own, gurgling, drowning in screams, stopping suddenly to look around then intensifying his squall. Everyone is gathered around the bed and I hear from within the circle, 'Don't call him "it".'

Yes, I've never stood above a grave but I have witnessed the birth of children.

After a late-night library trip I'd call her and say, 'Look at the moon.' Black boys rarely speak on the poet's muse so these twilight tropes seemed original – the moon is glowing new when seen through eyes deprived of cliché. She is bent over my windowsill – leaning out into the stars, a speckled blanket; if she reaches out it'll be ours. When I walk into a peace that was never going to last. Her hair – the carefully trimmed ends tinged with colours, one close inhale reminding me of home, of all the unknown black girls through hair care I've known – glows, a lustre unchallenged, then the jealous moon lights her up and dissolves the dimness of my room. It's all over her, she's illuminated, and this bath of light reveals her lack of garments. Our eyes see through the ceiling as we lie with hands interlocked, talking into the day when the sun will want its turn to watch, rays on us as we fall in love. She turns onto her stomach and places a hand on my stubble – like pins in her palm, a sensation running up her arm – draws me closer and I'm disarmed, and with a kiss we're surrounded by nothing.

Collecting sticks makes it more camp-like even though we have electric heaters to ward off unlikely but possible chills in the month of August. Four of us stand around the fire, one couple and two waifs oblivious to their future, the long souls of the fire creating clouds that will dissolve the next day, a smokescreen to the truth of gods blowing aerosols after puffs of their ambrosia. Bored numen lean on the sky and I see glittering stars as the pins and needles in their arms but the rest below, completing my circle, believe the universe's multiplying eyes are winking at us, giving their blessing to our eager bodies. We don't kiss, her bottom lip between my roof and tongue, making her numb like divinity, too many unconvincing cries make her a passive deity. Our Olympus is built with poles we thought we'd forgotten, and as we slide along our tent flooring, making sounds like an ocean stretching and withdrawing, I see cities aren't for me, that artificial lights create artificial love, and a love for our corner of the universe can never exist if you've never seen the stars. I wish I could walk through cities shooting out streetlights, bathing bodies with tender potential.

I'm sitting in the living room. The light from the TV is keeping the atmosphere alive. I can hear cats fighting through the downpour outside the window, a window I occasionally look out of, studying the rain sliding down the glass to be subsumed into the water at the bottom, slowly dissolving. She's asleep in our room, hers when she wakes, so I'll carry on sitting alone watching muted music videos until morning. An hour earlier, my nausea became bitter as I asked why she was sitting so close to me, dismissing her tired affection and turning my back on her. 'Golden Brown' played in front of us as she stared, hurt from what I hoped to heal from, trying her best not to give herself over to the rain outside the window. An hour earlier than this, I was stroking her back, fingers playing on her protruding spine, kissing the space behind her ears, licking it clean, but in time a Mau becomes a shorthair. I felt her sweating, knew she was uncomfortable, but kept her position to keep me in place. She said nothing, smiled as she adjusted her limbs. But I didn't move. So then, as the Stranglers sang on, she spun round on the sofa and ran to our room. So alone I sit, certain she never really loved me, her quick offence proof of what I always knew, watching a music video I don't recognise and a song I don't care to make out.

CONSTRUCTION

Anansi, your web is tender from the fingers that call you so I bring silk to help you weave your stories. There is enough for us both, so recreate my words and cover the sky with material the two of us will soon observe.

The letter starts by saying I seemed to show no signs of discomfort. There is a paragraph dedicated to my presentation, how well put together I was. No need for diagnosis or follow-up. I put the letter in the bin, walk to the fridge, open it, take out a bottle and drink. I always worry about my teeth when I do this, the damage I'm doing to them. A drip trails down my chin, parting my dark skin and splashing onto my white shirt. I move quickly. The bottle now wobbles, trying to steady itself on the side, no trace of the hand that clutched it, the hand now turning on the tap. After a few seconds of trying to sober up my shirt, I realise I've made it worse and know I have to change. Upstairs, I take off my jacket, hang it, unbutton my shirt from the centre; then I move on to the cuffs. Blood has soaked through one arm, cut and burnt, burnt sienna, a stain of shame, but no one will ever see it because my blazer never comes off. The Baileys would be an obvious blemish, like the alcohol on my breath. I grab my blue Extra and put them in my pocket. I take down a T.M.Lewin and decide to iron it out, noticing a slight crease just under the collar, a place no one looks. Blotches of red cover my bed, droplets trailing back to themselves. I've been meaning to change the sheets but the blood, being dry, coagulated, won't affect my shirt. I lay it down, careful not to add creases, and begin to iron, knowing how the shirt feels under the heat. There. Done. It looks good. Clean. Fresh. I put it on, then remember my drink, sure to use a glass this time, and a straw to protect my teeth.

Reading the symptoms felt like reading the traits of my sign – my understanding of mental health ailments was limited to depression and multiple personality disorder, and anything outside of this cinematic understanding sounded like an excuse for careless behaviour. I did wonder about the truth: where do I begin and BPD stops? – imagine living a life in which who you are feels like a prop. The printouts came eighteen years after I needed them, and watching my hand tremble with the page, the specialist reached out and told me the older I get, the fewer the traits. But for the bodies lying drained, piled up on the path to his office, this news has come too late.

With my eyes closed, I'm sliding my hand up and down my forearm, feeling the scars, the tribal marks, the conflict and human certainty, human suffering. And now you see. The stage lights can go off, a slammed door then darkness, light stripped of its difference, a black mass consuming my body. And here I stay until I can cut myself free. My lacerations are organised, straight lines ascending, an appeasement to the me who salivates at my life ending. How calculated is death, how careful with its scythe; does it wash its hands before and after taking someone's life? My hands are always clean when I remove the blade from its wrapper; I hold it in its centre and examine its edge. How sharp does it need to be to cause a single stroke of death? And is it sideways, or down the middle? My movie memory contradicts. It's either a horizontal line like Constantine or a vertical slit like John Wick. Is it death today or just a sign of emotional strain? I'll put the blade to my wrist until I pull it away. I know when I'm serious – when I can cut through my tats, something permanent disrupted – my reminders to fight, scrawled when I needed a lie to hold on to life. In cursive, *this too shall pass*, so I separate *too* from *shall*, then carve a line through 'Ozymandias'. The shock is like an icicle expanding in my chest; suddenly I can see my own breath. The left and the right arm bleed, obscuring what the rest of the tattoos read. Cross-legged on my bed, listening to the drip, watching the burgundy spread on my sheets. My old wounds itch – the feeling of scrambling pinpricks slowly mushroom out from the wound until three separated rivers of blood intervene to soothe. My failing cells cut loose. I never thought they'd be of any use. I wonder how long I will be like this – administering a tear with more care than I give to my own life.

4

My mum looks at the cuts on my arms and I can see her getting older. I know she's trying to translate English thoughts into Twi and struggling, so I put my hand on her shoulder and tell her not to worry. I'll be fine. 'What's tormenting you, son?' I explain, 'I'm a bit unwell, Mum. Nothing for prayers and paracetamol.' I appreciate her. I once watched her wrinkled stomach as she got dressed, examining the incision marking my first steps into fading light, my mother mutilated to guarantee my entrance. But when her eyes rest on my arms, slowly closing their openings, a slow blink, the rewinding frames of a flower blossoming, she gives in to the pressure to fall prostrate, presses her palm on her scar, splaying her fingers, as if full, as if she can't take any more, stopping something falling out. And she grieves.

Before bloodshed, a decision is made. Friends fold into strangers and instead of listening I'm counting the number of lines on each of my arms and which needs to be caught up, cut up. We carry on cutting up a few moments more, then I'm released to wonder about my release, if I have any antiseptic wipes left and the size of the plaster I'll need. I don't bleed onto the mattress any more as my mum is now familiar with the metallic smell of my plasma – giving credence to the idea I'm more machine than man. Lunch over, I sit at my desk and stare at what my GP described as 'the OCD-like neatness' of my cuts, some still worn as wounds, not there yet but on their way to scars. I squeeze them, measure them, run my finger over the callused ones, too wide so glued back together, too late for stitches; the doctor says the BioGlue helps reduce scarring. I've never been back. They scream attention in summer, so stunna shades with tints create a barrier between myself and assumptions. I'm told they're beautiful, described as battle scars or assumed to be tribal marks by awed onlookers unable to detangle their thinking from two-dimensional tropes. I don't wear my scars, they wear me; wear me down, wear me out, coerce me into increasing their number until they've won the war. Sometimes, I think I may just let them.

I wanted to live again. As they gathered, I felt the pressure of each tear awake to its own trickling sand weighing down the dirt on my grave. The torn tendons in my wrists stopped me from pushing against my choices, the bed where I lay. I wanted to know if they'd cry, if they'd weep, if they'd die – in another life my ashes are poured on distant rivers run dry.

It wasn't the demands of time that told me therapy was over, it was the gestures of arms exasperated by my self-loathing. 'Who taught you to hate yourself, K?', was said with a tremor like the slow and contained eddies on an unsettled river. I didn't know the answer but I knew I could never see her again. I left her therapy shack – a shed converted so a retiree could spend the last years of her life helping others to live theirs – unlocked my phone and deleted her number. The small amount of emotion in her voice was loud enough to scare me away, ear suddenly raised like those of suspicious prey. I couldn't burden my therapist or know I had the power to – so, therapist, I unburden you; yours was a shoulder that was supposed to stay dry. There are some people that you shouldn't see cry.

Baileys in hand, I thought a streetlight was the moon, so danced under the stilted lustre like the curve of a waning crescent pointed at the soles of my feet, imagining my other half two-stepping with me without symposiums, community centres only, knowing no one is compatible on Tottenham streets. And still, our steps are complete; and still, we find love.

The exterior of the pub changes more than the interior. There's a new chalked message on the board outside and this is enough to know I made it home yesterday. The same seats hold the same bodies and the same hands hold the same drinks. To find my place I order my usual and lean my elbows on the bar, resuming my role in this drunken masterpiece. I like to cut out irrelevant parts and end things quickly, so I sit with the Zimbabweans who drink like they're already dead. Our glasses stand on the table like trophies. My head falls on my interlocked fingers as my body slides the chair backwards, making me more comfortable as I watch, through a half pint, the distortion of my Zim friends talking about the superiority of the backsides back home. Standing by the only fruit machine in the pub is a girl who keeps looking over, the flashing lights behind her more arresting to my blurred vision than she is. She swallows the last drops of her drink. I imagine my fingers down there. And she'll return the favour, I know, throwing me up so there's space for another drink. A bell rings. We don't need any more but why not take advantage, grabbing what we might need to fall asleep. I look up at the roof. I mouth the words, 'I won't be sick.' Just get me home. I'm not drunk, I'm ill. My mum helps me into the house and sits on the edge of our tub while I'm choked by the rim of the toilet.

Sobs and sniffs sent us over to steady one of our own. My hand wouldn't rest directly on his shoulder but I tried to comfort him anyway. He was here often, looking out of place, almost too good for it, even though I knew he swapped clothes with the young boys on heroin. If you watched him long enough he looked like a crude addition to a painting long complete. I patted him on the back. His face rested on the bar, ears listening for drinks spilled on its wooden surface. His arms swayed beneath him, crossing the legs of the bar stool like pendulums. A glass of white wine and a glass of warm water stood by his head – his fortification in case someone tried to throw him out. 'It's all shit,' he muffles, 'Shit, man, it's shit.' I don't want to talk to him; I'm due to talk to myself this evening and my shit's had a longer wait. 'It's not all shit, bro. Swear. It gets better.' I give him another tap on the back and a see-you-next-Tuesday nod to the barmen and turn to leave. 'Is that your good deed for the day, K? A pat on the back and you've done your best? What shit.' He laughs, sounding like all his drink is sitting level in his chest, ready to spill when he's done, gargling with his levity. I haven't turned around. I'm two parts angry and three parts trembling, realising I've never given this man my name. But it's Edmonton, so a few seconds pass and I've shaken off the novelty and then, like I never wavered for a second, turn around and walk up to him, lowering my head so his space becomes ours, so close that my lips stroke the hairs on his ear and none around can hear me. I can smell the alcohol on his breath but the odour is bearable, almost neutral, and then, intoxicating. I start to feel like I've been smoking. 'How you know my name?' 'It's no secret, K.' My name again and I'm back to the cocktail mix I'd just shaken off. 'What the fuck is up with you, man?' 'Lost a bet that I won't hear the end of until eternity.' He raises his head for the first time and takes in the entire pub with a single look and blink. I feel he saw more than just the Zims, protected from home by their castle of glasses, the reclusive fruit machine which makes a noise every hour but gives up nothing else, the mistaken mating calls of the loud girls, the predators who don't need such invitations, and the ageing men, evidently made with care, who walk like the earth is moving too unsteadily beneath their feet, men who'll burst from their skin with a sudden movement, the local's locals, who have developed more friendship over silence and pints than we could appreciate. 'What a shithole,' he says to himself, grabs the glass of white wine and downs it in a few swallows, placing it back on the bar, the glass beaded with condensation. 'Look, bro, we all go through stuff. If you're at the bottom, then, you get me, yo . . .' 'Is that the best you can do?' he says 'Fuck me, I leave one place to get away from the lofty leanings of blinding cunts and end up in here with you.' 'Fuck this, I'm gone, man. I tried. Talk to God, bro. Maybe he can get you some new clothes.' I take a mouthful of his water and walk out, the bartender shouting about an unpaid orange juice. Inside the pub, the man, head back on his forearms, whispers, breathes the words, 'Talk to God . . .'

The footsteps on the shower surface stop abruptly and I watch Q walk out and dance to the music that silenced the stream, confident enough to move her arms freely to the oja instead of using right forearm to lift what most are embarrassed I'd see. She can't sing but her buzzing vocals, feigned Nigerian inflections and enthusiasm keep me listening and looking, imagining the tight cords of a gangan sounding around her and speaking of a traditional love. I lie in bed as drunk as she is but preferring the alcohol to stay level, enjoying the flow of a river of wine, red because she hates white, as it steadies inside me but undulates as I lift my head over my chest to keep my eyes on her moving and fusing with the tones of the only Fela left. A missed love language is watching your affection two-step, front to back, to a song on its fifteenth loop, and laughing – no sound, just your stomach moving – feeling the brisk brush of air out your nose as you half smile, the side of your lip upturned, genuine but still inauthentic; it all feels like a movie you've watched and accepted, a dreamy landscape being affected. But when she pauses the Prinz and puts her knees on the bed, an indent between my legs, her face an image my memory insists, and the sound of the springs is the only riddem left, the end of that tune is a climax that comes too soon, but as a child who claims he's sick, I enjoy the sweetness of the spoon.

It always takes her longer to get ready so I sit on the bed watching her applying, rubbing and straightening. I see myself in her mirror and notice how beautiful she is compared to me, how dark I am, how my skin is cursed: everlasting thirst, dry, and even from where I sit I can see the white worms piercing my pores. I smile to see my teeth, stained, so I swallow them again, my relaxed lips now wrinkled, reminding others of balm, aged after such a long-awaited stretch. I lower my head, eyes nearly rolling back trying to see the centre of my hair in the mirror. I notice the lonely area, curls no longer tight having developed a space between them. I drop my head further and close my eyes. I started shaving my head when the corners holding the line and weight of questioning age decided to, like I always do, step away from my face. I look up and avoid my own gaze, her make-up nearly done and as she brushes, blends or highlights, she smiles at me and asks if I'm all right, babe. I say yes. Then I tell her, 'I need a trim, man.' She understands. She turns to me, putting away her brush and pulling out wipes, the first white tissue coming out with a flourish, like a farewell to time, time she doesn't mind losing. 'Babe, we'll stay in today. Okay?'

I once dressed well but my suits no longer fit, abandoned in my wardrobe. This weight is new, a burden for bearers, as I once went shirtless in everything but the rain. Now, keeping myself alive takes more than raised dumbbells and bent knees with dead weight. Now belts have only one use ... One foot inside a leg, and without a struggle I capitulate to avoid chuckles, silent laughter from the side-splitting seams. Q loves my size and I try to smile when she jokingly calls me thick, stealing a glimpse as I walk past hotel mirrors and notice my thighs and behind, no longer smooth but dimpled, zaddy turned zuncle. As I unbutton, my thumb lifts what now spills over. We call it uncle belly. I call it antidepressants causing more problems than solving. I wish I didn't care, but soon, the tipping scales show I may not be here.

The gesture, the one that brings her into the genre of fiction, is the language of her body when smoking a cigarette – shoulders rolled in, head lowered while hands cup a lighter and neon tip from disapproving winds. Her inhale is to wield power, forcing the first speaker to wait for her answer while she blows smoke as if finally she can breathe. Waves of imitation about to break on us. I order us both another drink, complaining of the cold so we can sit inside. But then her wine glass supersedes her cigarette and I'm watching the rolling waters of her white wine as it lends itself to falsehood, the ornamental sip and glass raised halfway to the sky punctuating the end of each 'sophisticated' sentence.

Giving myself some space, serotonin to settle, sitting on the lid of a toilet seat with my palms on my temples, I notice the drip of a leaking tap is never out of time, off-beat, giving the porcelain it's bound to a melody: music to match moon-pulled seas contained by the ocean tubs of African deities. Then the drip becomes a tick to the flow of time, and I reach under the cold tap to preserve the trickle, freeze the hands for a moment, soak myself in the peace of nothing moving forward, just for a moment, just for a . . . The water spills over my palms and hits the tub loudly, shattering the surrounding air, signalling everything back in motion. I dry my hands and walk back into the countdown.

Saturday morning we collect videos and watch what we missed the night before. Sky sets are absent from all our homes so we stand level, equally excited to hear shattered glass or see elbow pads tossed to the crowd. Shops on the parade give us boxes we use as tables, and private property grass has no choice but to be our stage. I go through boxes, get hit by boxes, pinned on boxes, wide open on boxes. Excitement drives my hand into the enclosing wall and I use the blood to colour my forehead once cardboard becomes a chair.

I walk past our Costcutter, exchanging words with the shopkeeper arranging fruits. A response to my brother's age is cut short when he steps out in front of me, my old friend, my tag team partner, carrying the same boxes we once used for our Saturday morning title fights. He avoids eye contact. He's unshaven, with a blanket I know doubles up during the day as a coat to keep out the cold. I broke a pinky today and could give him the change; I put my hand in my pocket, hesitate, then walk on home, knowing I should turn back but not wanting to embarrass anyone to assuage my guilt.

Scales float to the surface of the tainted tea, wafers on the tongue but for the price of a new kettle I tolerate the calcified sacrament. The bag is drained till nothing is left and put aside to gather its strength, for in a few hours it will again be drenched. Use-by dates mean little as long as tops are green, so I pour regardless, cream-like thickness repulsing me more than a sour taste. Brown sugar because it's healthier, or so our house thinks, but still, we each heap five spoons to compensate for the melanin-tinged sweetness. I head back up to my room, so familiar with the steps I can focus on my next poem, not caring to stop the tea, peeking over the side, from spilling over and causing my favourite mug to weep. I reach the top – blowing, sipping, thinking – with a white page in mind: each letter I lay down a puzzle piece to spell out the images I imagine. Then I see her, side profile, lips moving with whatever I'd written, typed really, printed and stacked on my bed. My foot creaks on the final step, the stair knowing my intent was stealth but speaking under pressure. She drops the poem, the sheet floating back into the anonymity of the waiting pages. 'K,' my mum says. 'Don't write so much about me; you'll cry too much when I'm gone.' I didn't see her face when she spoke; she was my dream-like device, but now, sadly, I've awoke.

ACCEPTANCE

Nyame, I'm weak from calling you, from raising my voice with no rumble from the sky. I have starved, given away my stories with nothing but memories in return, a life hidden until I could show you my suffering. But my life means nothing to you, so I take my history and rise from the Golden Stool. Dua kontonkyikuronkyi na ema yehunu odwomſo.

I arrived at this ailment with no one trailing, no roses twirling, floating from my heels to dance with a gust sensing my scent, breeze stroking my neck, to land on a path directing people after me. They don't know what's wrong with me; tests and corrective lenses, failures, lip service to hope I was never going to engage with. Hope is a hand on a torn-up and beaten shoulder too used to Glasgow-kissing the floor, and as I cross my body to reach over and remove that liar's touch, the room takes the first steps towards our dizzy daily foxtrot. I drink to hope, each sip inspired by their prolonged absences. To everyone who has vanished or was never there to begin with. The diagnosis is damage to my brain, or chemicals not flowing the right way, or not existing, or tainted by secretion from an organ not supposed to bleed. The condition, I see the world as opposite: the day, bursting radiation from the sun, appears to me as night, and the evening, kept from swallowing itself by the alcoholic distraction of its inhabitants, never beamed so bright. When I wake, I pour a couple of drinks, sit by my window and look out into the dark horizon keeping Tottenham from escaping itself. My mum walks into my room and tells me it's 9am, put away the alcohol. I offer a glass and tell her to remember my condition in all exchanges with me. I pour her one, and another for myself, down both with a toast to misunderstandings, a solitary one as my mum left long ago. I sleep through the flickering old flame that was my day, coming alive during the night and spending most of my time drinking.

I'm watching the day through a breeze-blown slice in my curtains, obscuring nothing but my hour, summer and wind making peace, moving the leaves in the trees standing guard by my window, nervous after my attempts, the sun stroking fronds but leaving others in shadows, seeing the movement of the branches but hearing nothing but the serene sound of cars beyond the garden, limbs waving to me as a bird perches, maybe scouting for a house, onto the bough scratching the glass, knocking to bring me out into contentment while tiny flies shoot in and out of view, their quick existence something I could argue as I smell the fresh air through the dour scent of a depression that hasn't left my room in days, then swiftly feeling like I'm outside, alive and welcoming the wind to raise the hairs on my arms, a contrast that blossoms into hope.

I flush so adjacent cubicles won't hear the unscrewing top. This was my second trip to the WC, the first being an hour ago, 9 am, I think. The bottle's a leftover, a residue of a drunken evening – three hours' worth of juice because, as I shouted at the self-checkout the moment there was no doubt about the drought, it's ridiculous that supermarket chains so big don't sell alcohol before 10am. The neat gin burns my gums, cool on the tongue having so recently been brushed. There's no odour in the air to clash with the smell of alcohol but I can hear the resultant drops of early-morning coffees. My shoulders rise and fall as I feign childlike laughter to soften this image, breakfast on a throne, for those eyes we always perform to, we always feel looking. I peer up at the ceiling, floods ebbing, and remember when I once ran to the shop soaked by drifting rain, and looked up at a streetlight to notice that the water never touched its radiance. I turn the top and with dripping hands toasted a blinking lamppost about to fade out.

A line of brilliance cutting the centre of clouds – a god sailing across the pool of the sky. Light born of this streak creates a second life for sky-lined crystallised waters – purplish mountains, a natural design in the background belying the office buildings in front of them. From the sixth floor of the Southbank Centre I look on, a gin and tonic in hand, searching for inspiration in the water – water sparkling like ten thousand angelic tiptoes sneaking across the surface; water taking on the green of the trees leaning towards its exposure. Meals designed for wine surround me, but I toast the blood-red glasses with lemon in mine, lemon still hovering after so many drinks. Cyclists seem to race boats in the distance and tour buses slow to catch the view. Every day, I come here to sit, to turn my back on the world, to grow close to it again. And with every glass, it slowly becomes new.

I check my eyes in the mirror to make sure there are no puffs to give away what I've flushed, draining uninteresting small talk. I prefer to cry into the toilet so I can cleanse, feel I've sufficiently expelled my sadness. I sniff three times so there's nothing to notice when I walk out, a deep breath then a confident sigh when I deflate at my desk. It's 9.30 am and I've been here since 9. People start arriving. 'Good weekend?', someone asks. I slit my wrists on Sunday night. But what about you? 'Oh, that sounds great! I've been meaning to watch that for a while. I didn't do much. Just spent time with family. Something you'll be unable to do soon. And they won't miss you.' 'Yeah, I know what you mean. It can be jarring. But family time is important. We all say we hate them but we love them really.' 'True true.' I turn to my computer and let the weight of my face collapse, my eyes almost closed, the day just beginning. I open Outlook but turn off the monitor, my forehead hovering just above my desk. A hand on my shoulder, 'Let me guess, wild weekend?'

'I'm sure I cced you?' he says. He did, but not because he wanted to. Who would enjoy scrambling about for cultural references to make conversation? He knows how it would look if he didn't – the token black must be in hand at all times. 'My email isn't working properly, you know. Mad.' I answer. 'I can't tonight though.' Drinking with co-workers is a plunge into alcoholism that I'll need to deny to more than one person. So a day after an invite, last email sent, I look around and walk to the pub to take comfort as a loner, John O'Brian scribbling beside me. Today the office was more hostile than usual – I question, with my head down pretending to work, if I should engage, or they should. Everyone sips wine for the birthday moment as I turn down the last piece of chocolate cake. Food slows down the gin, anyway. I say goodbye to security but he ignores me. My girlfriend would say he didn't hear me, but I know how people are, and take a few steps to the pub. I've been thinking about the cinnamon trail I left from the toilet to my bedroom, the smell of spiced rum enticing more than vomit repulses. And then I see them. The work bunch, the black ones, drinking and laughing, running from the table and back as black people do, a good time being had by all. Except me. Panic or jealousy or envy – one of the three – turns me around before I'm noticed and I walk out the door. I haven't spoken to any of them since. They made me cry so now I'll never try.

Mel blows on his bullet before loading his handgun. He's beer-drenched and emotionally exhausted, tired of missing the wife who not only took her life but his. She's the air knocking his caravan door, the breeze guiding the napkin cleaning the barrel. He puts the gun to his head, rethinks, decides to swallow the bullet – poison if the shot fails – the bullet with one purpose, the one to drag him along with its speed to a place where his wife may be. He holds the gun in his mouth, muzzle flirting with the uvula hanging like a frozen pendulum, his thumb on the trigger, shaking, nervous, scared of what may come afterwards. He's hesitating, the movie score melding with the melodrama of the moment, and then, silence. He's given up but remains alive, crying at his weakness, staring, caressing the photo of his lost love. I watch this every night expecting a different outcome. Thinking – If guns were legal I would already be dead, and this scene would be rewatched by someone trying to understand why I did it.

I look around the reception. I'm feeling so isolated among so many that I have to reach over and calm my shaking hand. 'Dem Dey Go', the melancholy of the music steals the moment, piano keys pressing on a suffering note. The collective joy causes me to envy, to curl up thirsty. The couple leads an electric slide while I drink. Then I'm home, my brother holding onto my shirt, pulling it tight around my body; my mother stands by my door, anointing oil in hand, the language of her mind struggling to understand. I'm leaning out the window, heaving, breathing, feeling like I'm finally freed from solitary. I'm afraid to turn around – instead, I keep my eyes on the concrete beneath, imagining my fall – maybe two legs broken and no loss of consciousness at all. 'It's going to be cool, bro,' I hear from behind me. 'P,' I say, 'I just need some space.' 'I'm not letting you go, bro. It's going to be cool.' When I wake up he's asleep by my feet. I can't remember the sound of my brother's laugh. I always listen for it, as they listen for a key in my door, worry thundering floors as feet pace over and I'm told to keep my room unlocked. My brother's losing weight like I'm losing blood. He walks into my room and stops at my mattress. He stares at the multiple stab wounds, my blood in pockets all over the naked bed. He's never seen it with sheets off and all he can say is, 'rah'. He hasn't looked at me. He turns to leave and I ask is he okay? Why is he going, is it me? 'Nah,' he says, and closes my door. I sink to the floor. He once asked me if I think I can beat it; now he's sure I can't.

The seventh pill is absorbed in a wave of alcohol before I pick up my phone and call the only number my nurses seem to know. I suck in my bottom lip, ready to talk, a final taste of the spiced rum, an interlude to sobering up my conversation to appear sane to Samaritans . . .

They're okay to let me die – if I'm going to do it, there's nothing they can do. I hang up, hardened by the resolve I'll now have to show to dissolve my pride. I have to do it. I drink five more pills, Maker's Mark moistening the pathway into my diffusing body. I call my friend next, and ask her to sit on the phone with me while I die. She says okay so I hang up, nearly at the end. I take seven more quetiapine and call Q. 'I'm overdosing,' I say, 'I'm tired but I thought I'd call you.' Sleep is reaching for me and death has its grip on slumber's wrist. I feel drunk, talking about love and forgiveness and apologies and 'We could have been perfect together.' I pat down my bed but can't get it to release more pills, bounce my escape into my palm. 'K! K! This is not fair, can you please answer.' 'I'm here. Hey.' I'm thirsty. From my bed I reach down to pick up my drink but it spills, soaking the extension sockets. A worry for my books builds up then decays – any thought of what I love has the potential to delay, cancel my train of thought. I can't keep my eyes open, I tell Samaritans I'm falling asleep, tell my friend I'm dozing off, tell my ex I'll always be a votary at her feet. I'm weak, before I go, my last hope is that my mum doesn't find me.

An atheist in crowds, talkative, lyrical without conviction, discussions taking on the frayed edges of an intelligent conversation. As I walk home, doubting each step before I make it, I am agnostic. Before I close my eyes to sleep, I am a Christian. When I wake, pulled from the pool still reflecting the penumbra, I am spiritual, I am thankful, but I speak to myself, until I step out again onto shaky ground, cracked pavements, slabs broken in half with my step across their severance.

I'm sitting at a circular table next to a bookshelf I've tried to find comfort in, opposite my nurse, as she tells me about attachment theory. The old books had pages as brown as autumn leaves, crisp under my thumb, their details now falling from my mind as I dwell on cold visits, being caught while downstairs. The only people left to visit are the work well-wishers – my friends having dropped me out because they struggle to understand that sometimes my behaviour is not my own, disrupting their talk of accountability. This place, with its art-and-design-time drawings on the wall and wake-up calls for medication that leave us lined up in the halls, is purgatory – too sick for 'home' but not sick enough for the place where your identity could be swallowed by the moans. I wanted to be anywhere, anywhere away from sharp objects and full access to my pills. There were days when I'd fall asleep on my arm and wake up to see my wrist covered with the marks of a desperate escape, and I'd feel nauseous, struggling to understand my want of an exit. And in those moments, I see that, for now, this has to be the home for me.

When they visit, guilt overcomes everything and I'm forced to walk down two flights of stairs to sit with guests who knew of my decline before I shattered on our shared path. I refused one and heard nothing from them again, killing me before I could kill myself. Why does my mum come here, why does she pretend to care when this home is just a continuation of the first one she put me in? She's used to visiting me. Away. I want her to leave. 'Why are you looking at me, K?' I turn over to face the wall, my covers hanging off my bed and my arms as my pillows. My mum covers me up and whispers that I'll be okay. I should call her when I wake up.

I'm learning to play the keyboard. I mark the keys with different colours, the same therapy felts that seem to leak from the drawings around me, and put my phone where the music should be, using my trembling finger to take the YouTube video back to the start. I need a new prescription. For now, I ignore the tremors and keep the hallucinations to myself, seeing more time in here as worse than withdrawal. I come down to the recreational room every night, wave to the nurse who checks in, 'you not tired?', then try play accurately from memory. I know I'll never play perfectly from recall, even when my body is still, but still, I use the music to bring harmony to the passage of time.

I shake my head but he says this is for the best, 'go and get some water'. Before the kitchen I pass my mum, using two fingers to pull at and gauge the length of her hair, a gesture that ends immediately and she says, 'see K, look at my hair now, can I even do extensions.' I put my head down before the smell of cigarettes raises it again and my foster mum tells me, 'don't worry, dear, it'll be alright.' I walk into the kitchen, turn on the tap and pull a mug from the cupboard, ignoring who was already there, pretending I don't know the answer to the question of whether I work there. I wonder what I'm supposed to look like. Back in the room, he tells me he thinks I'm ready to self-medicate. I shake my head but he tells me it's for the best and hands over a box, shows me how to break one pill in half, though it's not ideal, they'll have the right dose soon. He'll be back next week to check on me. I drink the water and leave without saying goodbye.

My brother is supposed to visit. My mum sits on the only chair in my room and tells me about his new job, that he'll come when he finds time. He needs to make a good impression. I'm quiet so she gets up and starts cleaning up, stacking my books, asking if all this reading isn't responsible. Having family in here must be hard for him, my brother, something he needs to conceal from friends, tell them not to show anyone. Is this place helping or hiding me? My body requires a trigger warning, so even on hot days I wear full sleeves. The truth is blood across my wrists refusing to bleed out. Even when I'm fully clothed, my brother can see through me. No wonder he won't visit. I miss him and I'm sorry this happened to me, only because of how it's affecting him. I shouldn't be here. My mum finishes what she thinks is helpful and tells me about my dad's coughing fits. Both sick at the same time but she, fairly, tells me no one would look after him if it became serious. She sucks her teeth and rises to leave, having been here for hours and not seen me eat. She takes my keys and locks the door. 'I would,' I say. 'I would look after him.' I pull out a half-full bottle from under my bed and start separating my pills for the week.

ACKNOWLEDGEMENTS

First I would like to thank my incredible agent, Crystal Mahey-Morgan, the entire OWNIT! team, my friend and editor, Tom Avery, Elizabeth Uviebinené and Sam. I'd also like to thank the entire Adegoke family for always supporting and guiding me. Thank you Musa Okwonga for being a friend and the first person to believe in this book and thanks to everyone else who gave me feedback and editing notes: Kaleke, Candace, Korkor, Eden, Isaac, Alex, Leash, Kayo, Nii, Nels, Symeon and Clarissa. And thanks to my beautiful mother and my inspiring little brother.

RESOURCES

If you or anyone you know self harms or is struggling with suicidal thoughts, please contact the resources below:

CALM: https://www.thecalmzone.net/help/get-help/mental-health/

Mind: https://www.mind.org.uk/

Self Harm UK: https://www.selfharm.co.uk/

Harmless: http://www.harmless.org.uk/

Self Injury Support: https://www.selfinjurysupport.org.uk/

Recover Your Life: http://www.recoveryourlife.com/

Samaritans: https://www.samaritans.org/

Childline: https://www.childline.org.uk/